Spanish Missions

Risa Brown

Bethany, Missouri

Photo Credits:
Cover © Photodisc, Library of Congress; Title Page © Photodisc; Pages 5, 7, 15, 17, 19 © Library of Congress;
Page 9 © Gina Capaldi; Page 11 © Nancy Nehring; Page 12 © Glenn Frank, Library of Congress; Page 13 ©
Michael Blackburn; Page 21 © Endi Dewata; Page 22 © Blair Howard

Cataloging-in-Publication Data

Brown, Risa W.
    Spanish missions / Risa Brown. — 1st ed.
    p. cm. — (National places)

    Includes bibliographical references and index.
    Summary: Introduces the first Spanish inhabitants of America,
from why they came and daily life in the missions, to their affect on Native Americans.
    ISBN-13: 978-1-4242-1372-6 (lib. bdg. : alk. paper)
    ISBN-10: 1-4242-1372-X (lib. bdg. : alk. paper)
    ISBN-13: 978-1-4242-1462-4 (pbk. : alk. paper)
    ISBN-10: 1-4242-1462-9 (pbk. : alk. paper)

    1. Missions, Spanish—Southwest, New—History—Juvenile literature.
2. Southwest, New—History—To 1848—Juvenile literature. 3. Spaniards—
America—History—Juvenile literature. 4. Indians of North America—
Missions—History—Juvenile literature. 5. Missions, Spanish—California—
History—Juvenile literature. [1. Missions, Spanish. 2. Southwest, New—
History. 3. Spaniards—America—History. 4. Indians of North America—
Missions. 5. Missions—History. 6. Missions, Spanish—California—History.
7. Historic buildings.] I. Brown, Risa W. II. Title. III. Series.
    F799.B76 2007
    979—dc22

First edition
© 2007 Fitzgerald Books
802 N. 41st Street, P.O. Box 505
Bethany, MO 64424, U.S.A.
Printed in China
Library of Congress Control Number: 2006941003

Table of Contents

Spain in America

In 1492, Christopher Columbus and other explorers from Spain carried the hopes and dreams of their country. They came to America and wanted to **claim** the land for Spain.

COLUMBUS TAKING POSSESSION OF THE NEW COUNTRY.

The voyage had lasted 70 days (30 of which being lost by delay at the Canary Islands), from August 3 to October 12, 1492, when Columbus landed on the island called Guanahani by the natives, and named by him San Salvador. This island was rediscovered by the English, and by them called Watling Island. Columbus took possession of

Spanish Missionaries

Columbus returned to Spain to tell about America. Spain sent **missionaries** back to America to set up **missions**.

COLUMBUS AT THE COURT OF BARCELONA.

His reception, the most magnificent in all Spanish history, took place in February, 1493. He brought back with him from the New World six tattooed Indians, all sorts of animals, mineral products and vegetables, among others, Indian corn and potatoes, skins, weapons, household utensils, clothing, musical instruments and Indian baskets.

Soldiers

Soldiers went with the **priests** for protection while they looked for places to build their missions.

Building the Mission

The Spanish taught the Native Americans to build. The mission included kitchens, barns, workshops, sleeping rooms, and a beautiful church.

The Priest

V. R. DEL V. P. F. JUNIPERO SERRA

The priests were strong leaders. One famous priest, Junipero Serra, worked hard to build a group of twenty-one missions in California.

A Day in a Mission

Each day began with a church service. Then every person worked. Men grew food, took care of animals, or helped in the workshops.

15

Women sewed, made cloth and yarn, or cooked. Everyone had a job, even the children.

Conflicts with Native Americans

Even though the Native Americans learned a lot, they were not happy. They did not want to give up their **traditions**. There were many rules priests wanted them to follow.

19

Failure of the Missions

Many Native Americans died of diseases carried by the Spanish. Other Native Americans did not want to live near missions. Many missions closed and some fell apart.

Missions Today

Now missions are museums that teach about
the past and churches that serve their **communities**.

Glossary

claim (KLAYM) — to tell everyone that one country owns part of a new land

community (kuh MYOO nuh tee) — a group of people living together such as a town

mission (MISH uhn) — buildings used to teach and have church

missionaries (MISH uh ner eez) — a person who travels to a new place to set up schools and churches

priest (PREEST) — a leader in the Catholic church

traditions (truh DISH uhnz) — beliefs that are handed down

Index

FURTHER READING

Bowler, Sarah. *Father Junipero Serra and the California Missions.* Child's World, 2003.
Ditchfield, Christin. *Spanish Missions.* Children's Press, 2006.
Weber, Valerie J. *The California Missions.* Gareth Stevens, 2002.

WEBSITES TO VISIT

Because Internet links change so often, Fitzgerald Books has developed an online list of websites related to the subject of this book. This site is updated regularly. Please use this link to access the list: www.fitzgeraldbookslinks.com/np/sm

ABOUT THE AUTHOR

Risa Brown was a librarian for twenty years before becoming a full-time writer. Now living in Dallas, she grew up in Midland, Texas, President George W. Bush's hometown.